KNIGHTS OF RIGHT

Also by M'Lin Rowley

Knights of Right, book 1: *The Falcon Shield*
Knights of Right, book 2: *The Silver Coat*
Knights of Right, book 4: *The Fiery Gloves*

Visit us at ShadowMountain.com

Library of Congress Cataloging-in-Publication Data

Rowley, M'Lin.
The warrior's guard / M'Lin Rowley.
p. cm. — (Knights of right ; bk. 3)
Summary: Joseph, Ben, and Sam face werewolves and peer pressure as they continue their quest to become Knights of the Round Table by making the right choices.
ISBN 978-1-60641-240-4 (paperbound)
[1. Knights and knighthood—Fiction. 2. Werewolves—Fiction. 3. Conduct of life—Fiction. 4. Peer pressure—Fiction. 5. Time travel—Fiction. 6. Arthur, King—Fiction.] I. Title.
PZ7.R79834War 2010
[Fic]—dc22 2009049215

Printed in the United States of America
R. R. Donnelley, Crawfordsville, IN

10 9 8 7 6 5 4 3 2 1

KNIGHTS OF RIGHT

BOOK 3

THE WARRIOR'S GUARD

M'LIN ROWLEY

ILLUSTRATED BY MICHAEL WALTON

SHADOW
MOUNTAIN

1

THE BROKEN BRIDGE

"Aaahh! Joseph! Help!" ten-year-old Ben yelled to his older brother.

Joseph ran down the store aisle to see what was wrong. Just as he turned the corner, Ben jumped out, wearing a hideous Halloween mask.

"Ben! What did you do that for?" Joseph yelled in surprise.

Ben pulled off the mask, laughing so hard he almost couldn't breathe. "You should have seen the look on your face! I can't believe you were so scared!"

Joseph pretended to be interested in a row of costumes.

Ben continued, laughing. "Wait until I tell Dad you were scared by a kid's mask."

"Well, you shouldn't scare people like that—I thought the Black Knight had grabbed you or something. And you know what they say about the boy who cried wolf," Joseph replied.

Suddenly the boys' mom appeared with their little sister, Katie.

"Speaking of wolves," Mom said, holding up a big bundle of fake fur, "what about this costume, Ben?"

It was a suit made of shaggy brown fur, tattered jeans, and a ripped shirt. The hood had pointed wolf ears, and the hands and feet had rubbery claws.

"A werewolf!" Ben cheered, grinning. "I've always wanted to be one of those."

"So what am I going to be?" Joseph asked, glancing around at the costumes nearby.

"We'll find something good for you, too," Mom assured him. Then she looked at her watch. "Uh-oh—that might have to wait until later. I told Betty I'd be at the shelter in twenty minutes."

"But you don't usually volunteer on Fridays," Joseph protested.

"Yes, but they needed some extra help this week. October is a hard month to get volunteers because it's the beginning of the holiday season," she explained.

Their mom volunteered two afternoons a week at a center for abused women and children. Their dad was a doctor and did volunteer work, too. Both parents were concerned about helping other people. Joseph thought that was why they had agreed to let their sons become knights after they visited with King Arthur. He didn't know what King Arthur had said to his parents, but he was glad he could still earn his armor and become a Knight of the Round Table.

It was hard to believe that just two months earlier they had stumbled across King Arthur in a castle in the woods behind their house. The legendary king had traveled forward in time to find them. Joseph, Ben, and Samantha, their family's babysitter, had completed two quests so far and earned shields and chain mail. Now Joseph was eager for another quest.

"Look at this!" three-year-old Katie said,

tugging on Joseph's shirt. She held up a fluffy, pink princess dress with plenty of sparkles and flowers.

"Hey, Joseph, it looks like Katie found a costume for you," Ben teased.

Joseph made a face. "I wouldn't wear that for a million dollars," he said, pushing the dress away with the tip of a plastic sword he was holding.

"Hey, that's mine!" Katie pulled the costume close to protect it.

"Joseph, quit teasing your sister. Let's get moving, guys," Mom said. "And Ben, you still need to finish raking the leaves before you go with Sam to the football game tonight."

2

TO THE RESCUE

Ben was getting ready to jump into a huge pile of leaves when True Heart flew over, squawking.

"What's wrong, T. H.?" Ben asked.

Joseph and Ben exchanged excited glances, realizing it was True Heart's signal that King Arthur wanted to talk to them. After telling Sam, their babysitter, where they were going, they gathered their shields and chain mail and hurried into the woods.

Things were strangely quiet as the boys followed True Heart through the trees. They didn't meet up with the Black Knight or any of his henchmen. But when they got to the castle, they saw immediately that something was wrong. Pieces of the outer wall were crumbling, and there was a huge hole near the drawbridge. Joseph and Ben gaped at it in shock. Then they realized that the drawbridge wasn't lowering itself automatically as it always had before.

"This isn't good," Joseph said.

The boys stared at the empty hole for an instant and then at the empty woods around them. At least they hoped the woods were empty.

"King Arthur!" Ben yelled. "Are you in there? Are you okay?"

There was no answer.

"We'd better go back and get help," Joseph suggested.

Ben agreed. The boys raced back to their house and burst through the front door.

Sam looked up from the book she was reading to Katie. "What's going on?" she asked. "Is everything okay?"

"No!" Ben cried. "We got to the castle, but the drawbridge won't open, and there's a huge hole in the castle wall!"

"That has to mean King Arthur is hurt," Joseph added.

"Or worse," Ben gulped.

Sam looked worried. She rushed into the kitchen and returned with a first-aid kit.

"That's a good thing to take with us, but how are we going to get into the castle?" Ben asked.

"Your parents have some rock-climbing equipment in the garage. That might help you get across the moat," Sam said thoughtfully. "Maybe I should come with you."

"Then who would watch Katie? Besides, what if a monster shows up?" Joseph asked.

"Hey, who defeated the last one we saw?" Sam objected. Then she sighed. "But you're right. I need to stay here with Katie. Just be careful. And hurry back when you find out King Arthur is okay. Remember, we're going to the football game tonight."

Ben got one of the climbing ropes from the garage, and the two boys hurried back through the woods to the castle.

"So, how do we do this?" Joseph asked, uncoiling the rope. One end was already tied in a loop. The knot looked sturdy, but

Joseph hadn't learned much yet in Boy Scouts about knots, so he didn't know for sure. The moat looked pretty scary, especially since he couldn't tell how deep it was or if there were any ferocious creatures in it.

Just then True Heart swooped down, snatched the rope from Joseph, and flew toward the castle.

"Hey! Come back with that!" Joseph yelped.

Ben laughed.

True Heart dropped the loop around a spike at the top of the drawbridge and flew the other end back to Ben.

"Cool!" Ben grinned, getting ready to jump.

Joseph stopped him. "What are you doing? That spike could break under your weight!"

Before Ben could answer, something

whistled past Joseph's ear and landed in the moat. A black arrow bobbed to the surface.

Ben and Joseph looked at each other in shock.

"We'll be shot full of holes if I don't try," Ben shouted. Holding tight to the rope, he took a few steps backward and then ran toward the castle, yelling like Tarzan.

Joseph looked over his shoulder into the woods to see the Black Knight running through the trees toward the castle. As Ben landed in the courtyard beyond the moat, Joseph swallowed nervously, trying not to look behind him. He hopped up and down anxiously while True Heart flew the rope back to him.

Another arrow glanced off the castle wall.

"Hurry up!" Ben hollered.

Joseph copied his brother's running jump, only without the yelling.

Landing with the first-aid kit tucked under his shield was hard work, and Joseph hit the ground with a thump.

Ben helped him up, and they ran for the door across the courtyard. Arrows thudded into the ground nearby.

"I think he's a better shot this time," Ben yelled to Joseph.

"He was always a good shot," Joseph

argued. "But there was some force that kept him away from the castle and away from our house. It's a good thing we have our armor now!"

As if to prove his point, an arrow hit his shield and bounced off.

The boys skidded to a stop in front of the door when it didn't automatically open. Ben pounded on it. "Open up! Hello! We're getting shot at out here! Help us!" he yelled.

"I don't think King Arthur can hear you." Joseph gasped as an arrow pierced the door right next to Ben's hand.

"Wait a minute!" Joseph grabbed the door handle and pulled. The door opened easily.

"If you'd given me a second, I could have figured that out," Ben huffed.

Joseph laughed. But he stopped laughing

when an arrow landed between Ben's feet. The boys ran inside the castle, slamming the door shut behind them.

At the far end of the throne room, King Arthur sat on his throne.

"What happened? Are you okay? Why wouldn't the drawbridge open?" Joseph asked worriedly. "Can the Black Knight get in here?"

"No, it's not quite like that," King Arthur said, giving them a reassuring smile. "I'm glad both of you are all right. You see, I usually use Merlin's magic to control the drawbridge, but after the troll appeared, Merlin and I realized we would have to change our strategy. The woods are dangerous enough with the Black Knight, but they are deadly with a troll on the rampage. Do you know the troll even threw boulders at the castle walls? He did some damage before I could stop him."

"I wonder where he learned that trick," Ben joked, remembering how Sam had thrown rocks at the troll.

"It's not funny, Ben," Joseph whispered reprovingly. Aloud he asked, "Are you going to be all right, Your Majesty?" as he set the first-aid kit on a nearby table.

"Ah, yes. Do not worry about me. I have the might of right on my side. Now, instead of using Merlin's magic to control the drawbridge, I use the magic to keep the troll out of trouble. "

"You can do that?" Ben asked eagerly. "Can you use him to scare my teacher into not giving us so much history homework? I bet we wouldn't get any homework if a troll showed up!"

"Ben!" Joseph scolded.

King Arthur laughed. "I'd prefer to keep the troll safely out of sight, Benjamin. But if you need help with history, perhaps I can be of assistance. Fidelis and I come from the very pages of history, don't we, boy?"

He patted the dog's head. Fidelis barked cheerfully and licked King Arthur's hand.

"Fidelis? Is that his name?" Joseph asked.

"Yes. *Fidelis* means 'loyal' or 'faithful' in Latin. And Fidelis is an exceptionally loyal dog." Arthur smiled down at his dog and then looked back at the boys apologetically. "I'm afraid I don't have time for a story today. I need to confer again with Merlin about how best to use his magic. I must wish you luck on your quest without the help of a tale."

"Will you be okay in here by yourself?" Joseph asked worriedly.

"I will be fine. The most important thing is for you to earn the next piece of armor as quickly as possible. And I will train Fidelis to let down the drawbridge for you the next time you come."

"That would be the coolest dog trick ever!" Ben exclaimed. "I'll bet Fido can do it, too! Is it okay if I call him Fido?"

"I think perhaps it would be best just to call him Fidelis for now. *Fido* means 'I trust.' To call him Fido, you have to show him he can trust you."

"But he can trust me!" Ben protested.

"That is easy to say, but trust is something you have to earn. A long time ago, Fidelis had a master who betrayed his trust. It takes time for him to learn to trust others now," King Arthur explained sadly.

"What happened?" Joseph asked.

"That is a story for a later time. For now, you boys have a quest to undertake, and I have a wizard to speak to. Merlin is not happy with me if I'm late." King Arthur smiled and waved good-bye.

3

THE CLUES

The boys nervously swung back over the moat. True Heart retrieved their rope and then led them on a zigzag path through the woods. The falcon seemed to know what he was doing because they never saw the Black Knight, and soon they could see their back fence through the trees.

Before they reached it, however, True Heart swooped down and picked something out of the bushes. It was dirty white streaked with gray and looked like some type of fur.

"What is that?" Joseph asked.

"I dunno," Ben shrugged as True Heart dropped the object into Joseph's hands.

"It looks like sheepskin," Joseph said. "What kind of clue is this?"

"It's a warning that we're going to meet some haunted sheep on Halloween. Baah!" Ben laughed, walking around like a zombie.

True Heart cocked his head and looked at Ben as if that was the most ridiculous thing the falcon had ever heard.

Joseph picked the twigs out of the wool as they followed True Heart to the fence.

"Maybe they're man-eating sheep," Ben suggested. "Or ghosts of the lamb Mom always makes us eat. Ick!"

"I like lamb," Joseph defended. "And we don't have to face man-eating ghost sheep."

"Are you sure?" Ben asked.

Joseph just shook his head at his brother.

Sam and Katie were putting the rest of the leaves into a bag when the boys climbed back over the fence. "Is King Arthur okay?" Sam asked worriedly.

"The troll is as crazy as you are, Sam," Ben laughed. "He threw rocks at the castle and damaged the wall."

"What?" Sam gasped.

"King Arthur took care of it," Joseph explained. "I don't think we'll have to worry about the troll for a while."

"That's scary, but I'm glad King Arthur's okay." She sighed in relief. "What's that in your hand? You're not going to knit a sweater, are you?"

"Uh, no." Joseph offered her the wool. She rubbed it, looking puzzled.

"A clue?"

They all shrugged. Joseph told her how King Arthur had been too busy to tell the story this time, so they had to figure things out completely by themselves.

"Okay, let's think about this sheepskin. I think I heard of some evil, man-eating sheep in Greek mythology," Sam said thoughtfully.

Ben laughed and Joseph rolled his eyes.

"Not you, too! I thought you were smart, Sam!" Joseph groaned.

Sam and Ben laughed, and Ben gave her a high five.

"Hi, I'm home!" Mom called out the back door. Everyone rushed back inside to greet her. "Thanks for watching the kids for me, Sam."

"It was no problem," Sam said.

Their mom had a bunch of grocery bags in her arms, and they hurried to help her unload them onto the counter. Ben lifted out a bag of flour, one of sugar, some baking powder, and some spices and other things he didn't recognize.

"What are you making?" he asked.

"I'm going to make an apple pie," Mom answered. "Would you get me a couple more apples from the basket in the garage?"

Ben and Joseph raced to the garage while Sam helped put away the rest of the groceries. True Heart reached the basket first and picked up an apple, dropping it on Ben's head. Ben picked it up off the ground.

"Ooh, this one's all rotten!" He made a face at the brown, squishy apple. "Why'd you pick this one, T. H.?"

"Maybe it's a clue!" Joseph realized.

They grabbed a few apples—none of the others looked rotten—and went back inside. Sam didn't know what this clue meant, either, but Mom gasped when Ben showed her the rotten apple. "Was this one with all the others?"

"Yeah, why?"

"Oh, no! One rotten apple can ruin the whole bushel!" she groaned. "I need to check more often to make sure they don't go rotten like that."

"None of the others looked bad," Joseph reassured her.

"Well, hopefully we caught it in time," she said. "Now, who wants to help me make a pie before you kids go off to the football game?"

They were just rolling out the pie dough

when Katie started flapping her arms and running around the room. "I a birdie, Mommy!" she announced. "I a birdie!"

"That's nice, sweetheart," Mom said.

The boys ignored Katie until they heard a tapping sound on the kitchen window. True Heart was at the window, trying to get their attention. Ben and Joseph looked out, and their jaws dropped. The backyard was covered with birds. Most were crows and blue jays, but there was even another falcon like True Heart, and Joseph saw an owl swoop onto their tree house. Feathered creatures flew all across the backyard.

"I guess that's the last clue," Joseph whispered.

"T. T.'s friends! Tweet, tweet!" Katie said, swooping around the room.

“T. H.,” Ben and Joseph corrected together. T. H. was the nickname Ben had given True Heart when he decided the falcon’s real name was too long.

Mom and Sam looked out the window at the birds.

“Sheep’s wool, apples, and birds. What do you think it all means?” Joseph asked.

“It means we are going to have a really messy lawn,” Mom sighed.

Ben and Joseph laughed.

4

FOOTBALL QUEST

By the time they got to the high school for the game, the stands were packed. Samantha saw her friend Lizzie at the top of the bleachers, so the boys tromped up the metal steps behind her. A group of teenagers crowded together in the corner of the top bleacher, laughing and cheering loudly.

"Well, look who it is! Samantha!" Jordan cheered, and then he hiccupped.

Sam waved back, but she frowned. Jordan sounded as if he'd been drinking. Then she saw beer cans at their feet.

Ben and Joseph glanced at each other nervously.

"What are you guys doing?" Sam asked.

"We're watching our team kill the other guys!" Lizzie laughed. "What do you think we're doing?"

"No. I mean, Why are you drinking?" Sam asked worriedly.

"Hey, it's not like we're gonna get caught! Nobody cares," one of the boys argued. His words were slurred. "Want a beer? We could even let your friends there have some. What do you say? You boys want a beer?"

"I can't believe you're doing this!" Sam gasped, glancing back at Ben and Joseph. "You're drunk! I don't drink, and neither do they. Drinking kills brain cells. You are living proof of that. And drinking and driving kills people. We're leaving."

"Well, if you aren't going to have fun with us, then we don't want you here," Jordan said angrily.

"You think you're too good for us or something? What kind of friend are you?" Lizzie complained to Sam.

Sam frowned. "Maybe I should ask you the same question. What kind of friend tries to get me to drink? What kind of friend tries to get a ten-year-old to drink? In fact, what kind of friend drinks at all? I'm going to tell the principal so you guys can get some help. That's what real friends do."

Sam turned away as Jordan stumbled to his feet and yelled, "You aren't going to tell anybody!" Then he pushed her.

She fell with a loud clatter and slid down the bleacher steps.

"Sam!" Joseph yelled. The boys rushed down the steps to her, but Sam scrambled quickly to her feet, brushing off a shiny silver breastplate that had protected her in the fall.

Joseph and Ben cheered when they saw the armor and gave her a high five.

Lizzie came up behind them. "Wait, Sam," she said. "I think I'm ready to go."

Jordan swore and called the girls names. Sam and Lizzie ignored him and followed Ben and Joseph to the parking lot.

"Thanks, Sam," Lizzie said shyly. "I was embarrassed you caught me up there drinking. I took only a sip or two, but I felt so bad.

I was afraid to say no. I didn't want the guys to make fun of me. I should have said no."

"I can't believe you let those boys talk you into it. What happened to the Lizzie I know, the Lizzie who would never let a guy push her around?" Sam asked.

"I thought they were my friends. I wanted them to like me." Lizzie shrugged and sighed. "But when they acted like jerks and Jordan pushed you, I realized my real friend was walking away."

Sam gave Lizzie a hug. "Good friends help you do good things. You guys remember that," she said to Ben and Joseph. "Lizzie, these are my friends. I babysit their little sister. Ben and Joseph and I hang out together."

Lizzie shook the boys' hands. "You're lucky to have a friend like Sam."

"We know." Ben shrugged and grinned. "She's wicked awesome against trolls."

"Jordan is a troll, isn't he?" Lizzie sighed.

Ben, Sam, and Joseph shared a grin.

5

BUSTING BOREDOM

"We should do something," Joseph said. His friend Chase agreed.

"But what is there to do?" Steven sighed.

The three boys sat on the back porch of Steven's house, watching leaves fall off the trees. It wasn't very exciting, especially after the excitement of the football game the night before.

"We could play football," Chase suggested. Steven and Joseph groaned. They'd been playing football all week, every day after school. Chase never seemed to get sick of it, but Joseph and Steven were tired of football.

"What about baseball?" Steven suggested. "I have my ball and bat in my room."

Joseph and Chase nodded, and Steven ran to get his stuff.

One of the boys hit the ball with the bat, while the other two chased after it. Chase hit a sweet line drive that sent Steven and Joseph scrambling down the street. Joseph got the ball first and turned to toss it to Chase.

But Chase had picked up a pumpkin from someone's front porch. He swung the bat at the pumpkin, smashing it to bits and sending pulp and seeds all over the driveway.

"Nice hit," laughed Steven. He grabbed the bat and smashed another pumpkin. Then he tossed the bat to Joseph. Joseph caught the bat but shook his head.

"It's your turn, Joseph!" Chase urged.

"Joseph steps to the plate to score the winning run in Pumpkin Smash Ball!" Steven said in his best sports-announcer voice.

"I don't think it's a good idea, guys," Joseph said.

"It's okay! No one will know," Chase said with a grin. "The secret stays with the three of us, right?"

"This isn't a good secret. We are destroying other people's property and making a mess." Joseph shook his head. "You're my friends, right?"

"Yeah," Steven said.

"Then let's go knock on the door of this

house, tell them we're sorry, and clean up this mess," Joseph said.

Chase and Steven looked at each other and then slowly nodded. They followed Joseph up the steps. Joseph did most of the talking, but Steven and Chase helped clean up the pumpkins.

It wasn't until the boys headed back to Steven's house that a shiny silver breastplate appeared on Joseph's chest. "Sweet! I passed the test," Joseph said to himself. He thought he'd said it quietly, but Chase heard him.

"What test?" he asked.

"Nothing," Joseph said quickly, but Chase's eyebrows rose. "Well, promise you can keep a secret?"

"You bet," Chase nodded. Steven came over as they stopped on the sidewalk.

"King Arthur made me a knight, and I just earned a piece of armor for making a good choice," Joseph confided, grinning when his friends looked skeptical.

"Is it a video game or something?" Chase asked.

"No, it's real."

"Then where's your armor?" Steven asked.

"You can't see it, but it's right here," Joseph said, and he tapped on his breastplate. "Go ahead, hit me with the bat."

Steven's eyes widened. "You're not serious!"

"I *am* serious! Hit me!"

Steven swung gently and tapped Joseph on the chest.

"I didn't even feel it," Joseph grinned.

Chase swung the bat a little harder.

"Oomph," Joseph puffed, but the blow didn't hurt him.

"Cool! How'd you do that, man? I wish I had armor!" Chase said.

The boys laughed and hurried to Steven's house.

6

RIDE RIGHT

Ben looked down at his scraped knees with disgust. He was at a skate park with a group of friends, but he wasn't exactly skateboarding. He was just trying to stay balanced on Tony's skateboard for more than five seconds. Tony, his best friend, watched him and laughed. He was trying to teach Ben some tricks, but it wasn't working.

"It's okay, Ben," Tony said. "Stick with the pro, and I will have you doing a kick flip in no time."

"Hey, I want to teach Ben something,"

Jake cut in. "Ben, want to learn how to fly? I dare you to skate down the hill and off this launch ramp right now."

All the boys stopped what they were doing. Some of them laughed. Jake was always daring kids to do stupid things.

Ben kicked the ground in frustration.

"Are you crazy?" Tony protested. "Ben isn't ready to go off the launch ramp yet. That's for expert riders."

"Fine," Jake said, glaring at Tony. "Ten bucks says Ben can't skate off this little tiny launch ramp."

Ben bit his lip and stared at the ramp. It was pretty high. Anyone going off it would fly—and then fall pretty hard.

After a few seconds, Jake flapped his arms and made bird noises. "Ben's just a big chicken—all talk and no action. I should have known he wouldn't do it." He laughed. "Would any real men like to take my bet?"

Ben wondered briefly what Joseph or Sam would do in this situation. He didn't have to think very hard. Taking a deep breath, he turned to face Jake. "Thanks anyway, but I don't feel like flying in an ambulance today. Maybe I'll ride that ramp later, but for now I'm kind of fond of keeping all my blood in my body and all my bones in one piece."

"Yeah," Tony laughed. "Remember when Jake fell off the monkey bars in the second grade and fainted at the sight of his own blood? We wouldn't want Jake fainting when we have to scrape Ben off the pavement. Come on, guys, let's go to Ben's house. Maybe we can get T. H. to catch a mouse."

Ben smiled as the group nodded and turned to go. Jake scowled but didn't say anything.

"Thanks, Tony," Ben whispered. He smiled even wider when he realized he was wearing a shiny silver breastplate. He had made a good choice, and he couldn't wait to show his new armor to Joseph and Sam.

In that instant Ben tripped on Tony's skateboard and landed facedown on the sidewalk. Thankfully, his breastplate prevented a sharp rock from jabbing his chest.

"I really need to teach you how to ride that thing before you kill yourself," Tony laughed, helping Ben to his feet.

Ben just grunted. Knights didn't need to ride skateboards.

7

ATTACK

"Chain mail, a shield, *and* a breastplate!" Ben cheered as he, Joseph, and Sam followed True Heart through the woods. It was late afternoon on Saturday, and big dark clouds were blocking the sun. But Sam wasn't babysitting, so they had decided now was the best time to visit King Arthur and show him their new armor.

"Yep, we're certainly moving along quickly," Joseph agreed, admiring his new breastplate. "Who knew it could fit so well? My history teacher said knights' armor was awfully uncomfortable, but this doesn't feel bad at all!"

"Must be magic," Sam said.

"Well, my magic isn't working very well, because my breastplate's a little too big. Sometimes it comes all the way up to my chin," Ben complained.

Joseph and Sam laughed. Then Sam pointed through the trees.

"Hey, is that the castle? It looks so cool!"

"It is cool," Joseph and Ben agreed. "Even with all the holes in it!"

Just as they reached the crumbling castle wall, the drawbridge started to lower and Fidelis ran out, barking.

"Look who let down the drawbridge! Fidelis is awesome," Ben grinned. "Are you happy to see me, boy?"

"His bark doesn't sound very happy," Joseph said uneasily.

"He's not here to greet us," Sam said in a strange voice. "He's here because of them."

The boys turned to look as three huge animals came into view between the trees. They were bigger than any dog the kids had ever seen, with tattered, dirty black fur and huge bloody teeth. One of them howled, and the sound sent shivers down the kids' spines.

"Wolves? In our forest?" Joseph choked out.

"Those don't look like normal wolves," Sam gulped.

All three of them glanced up to see the full moon peeking through the clouds. "Werewolves," they gasped as Fidelis raced past them, growling and snarling.

The werewolves sprang into action. They bit and clawed at Fidelis until his flanks were slashed and bleeding. But he kept fighting.

"Hey, you stupid mutts! Get away from King Arthur's dog!" Ben yelled.

Two of the werewolves turned toward the kids. Joseph swung his shield and hit one in the face just as it lunged at him. It lurched to the side and attacked Sam instead. But its claws screeched uselessly across her breastplate.

The second one went for Ben, its huge jaws closing around his neck.

"Joseph!" Ben hollered.

Joseph banged his shield down on the werewolf's head, and it jumped away.

"Did it bite you?" he gasped.

"No. Good thing my breastplate is too big." He sighed with relief.

Joseph snorted as he looked around. Fidelis had apparently wounded the werewolf he was fighting, because it was lying still on the ground. But Fidelis had collapsed next to it.

The werewolf that had attacked Ben howled and rushed at Fidelis. The third werewolf followed him.

"We have to get Fidelis to the castle before they kill him!" Ben yelled. "Get away from that dog, you monsters!"

Sam threw rocks at the werewolves to distract them, and they started after her.

"Joseph!" Sam yelled.

"Get Fidelis! I'll meet you at the castle!" Joseph yelled back. He raced into the trees, drawing the werewolves after him.

True Heart swooped down with a piercing screech and attacked the werewolves from the air.

Ben and Sam pulled Fidelis onto Sam's shield and dragged him toward the castle. Joseph caught up with them, throwing rocks he scooped off the ground as he ran.

They made it across the drawbridge with True Heart attacking both remaining werewolves. Then, before the werewolves could get onto the bridge, Joseph, Ben, and Sam drew it up. True Heart flew over the castle wall as the werewolves howled angrily.

8

EARNING TRUST

“Fidelis is hurt!” Ben yelled as they dragged the shield into the throne room.

King Arthur rushed toward them.

“He was bitten by werewolves. Do you think he’ll become one?” asked Joseph, worriedly.

“No, I do not think he will,” King Arthur assured them, kneeling down next to Fidelis. “A werewolf bite doesn’t affect animals the same way it does humans. His wounds are many, but they are not deep. He is a skilled fighter.”

King Arthur still had the first-aid kit Sam had sent with the boys on their first visit, so Ben ran to grab it.

"You must be Lady Samantha." King Arthur smiled at Sam as he cleaned and bandaged Fidelis's wounds.

"Yes. It's an honor to finally meet you, Your Majesty," she said.

"The honor is mine," he responded. "You children have all been very brave tonight."

"How did the werewolves get here?" Ben asked.

"I suppose the same way the troll did. I'll have to use more of Merlin's magic to see if I can contain the werewolves as well. Perhaps we can discover how the Black Knight is finding a way to bring his followers here. Little by little he is building up his army,"

King Arthur said sadly. "But thankfully, there is hope. You, my young knights, give me that hope. So, what did you learn this time?"

"Well, I guess the clues were pretty easy," Joseph said, but he realized he should have paid more attention to them. "The sheep wool was, um—well, the rotten apple meant—that is to say, the birds . . . Well, maybe they weren't so easy. All I know is, we earned these breastplates."

They all laughed.

"Perhaps if I told you the story of Fidelis the clues would make more sense," King Arthur suggested.

Joseph and Ben nodded eagerly, and Sam looked excited. It was her first time hearing a story straight from King Arthur.

First, King Arthur carried Fidelis to a bed

in another room and then returned to the throne. Ben, Sam, and Joseph sat on the floor in front of him.

"As I promised, my story is about our friend Fidelis," King Arthur began. "Fidelis belonged to a shepherd in the fields near Camelot. He was an intelligent and loyal dog whose job was to herd the sheep and protect them from wolves. Imagine the shepherd's surprise late one afternoon when Fidelis attacked one of the sheep. The shepherd pulled him back, yelling angrily. When he finally let Fidelis go, the dog attacked the same sheep again.

"The shepherd was enraged. He chained Fidelis to a tree in the woods and left him there when he led the sheep home for the night. While the shepherd was asleep, a wolf attacked the flock, killing every sheep as they

huddled in the barn for the night. Fidelis was not there to raise the alarm or save them.

"How did the wolf get in the barn, you may ask? The wolf had been among the sheep all day, disguised by a coat of magical wool. Fidelis could smell his true identity and had attacked the wolf in sheep's clothing to warn his master."

"Wow!" said Ben. "I think I've heard that saying about a wolf in sheep's clothing before. Fidelis is an awesome dog! That shepherd must have been sorry."

"Fidelis is a truly good dog, Benjamin. But I think you mean Fido, don't you?" King Arthur asked with a smile.

"You mean—" Ben's face lit up excitedly. "We can call him Fido?"

"I think he can trust you now, all of you," King Arthur nodded.

Ben pumped his arm, Joseph laughed, and Sam grinned.

"So now we know what the sheep wool meant!" Joseph said. "The wolf pretended to be a sheep until he could eat them. Is that like kids who pretend to be your friends but try to get you to do bad things that can destroy your life?"

"Exactly." King Arthur smiled. "And what about the other clues?"

"Well, remember your mom said that one bad apple can spoil the whole bushel. So maybe one bad friend can make the whole group go bad," Sam suggested.

"I know how that goes," Ben remembered. He was glad he hadn't listened to Jake.

"And the birds?" Joseph frowned.

"The birds were T. H.'s friends!" Ben cut in.

"'Birds of a feather flock together,'" Sam said. When the boys looked at her in confusion, she explained, "It's a saying. It means you go with friends who are most like you."

"Very good, Samantha. If you wish to be a good knight, you need good friends," King Arthur said. "Now, another name for a breastplate is a guard. Good friends are like guards to protect you. Without loyal friends, a knight is in danger. If you do not have friends who help you become knights, you won't succeed. Fidelis is lucky to have friends like you."

"And we're lucky to have a friend like him!" Ben agreed. "Otherwise we'd be werewolf chow!"

They all laughed again.

9

KING BEN

Joseph finished writing the note to his parents and read it out loud to make sure it was okay.

"Dear Mom and Dad,

"We are all fine, and we'll be home very soon. King Arthur's dog, Fidelis, was injured, so we are staying for a little while to make sure he's okay. He is starting to do better, so that's good.

"I love you,

"Joseph."

He finished reading and looked up at Sam to see what she thought.

"Sounds good," she nodded.

Joseph rolled up the note and then handed it to True Heart.

"Will you take this to my parents, T. H.?" he asked hopefully.

T. H. chirped and flew off, the scroll in his claws.

"Guys! Fido rolled over so he could eat," Ben said excitedly, running in from the other room. "And look! King Arthur has some swords he says we can practice with for a while."

"Cool!"

Sam and Ben each took a sword. Joseph grabbed one as well, just in time to block a swipe from Ben.

"Hey!" Joseph squeaked in surprise. "I wasn't ready."

"I don't think the Black Knight would care if you were ready or not," Ben teased.

Joseph swung at Ben, who ducked just in time. They laughed and swung at each other again.

A few seconds later Joseph was hit on the leg. "This is dangerous!" he yelped.

"You okay?" Sam asked worriedly.

He laughed and swung back at her.

They practiced with the swords until they got tired. King Arthur was still with Fidelis in the other room, but he had left his crown and scepter on his throne.

Ben picked up the scepter and turned it over in his hands. Then he grabbed King

Arthur's crown, plunked it on his head, and sat down on the throne.

"You there." He pointed the scepter at Joseph. "What are you doing, you lazy boy? Fetch me my food! And you, girl! Get me my royal robes! This sitting around is unacceptable!"

Sam laughed. "Certainly, Your Majesty."

"No way!" Joseph protested. "We want King Arthur! Down with King Ben!"

"Down with King Ben! Down with King Ben!" Joseph and Sam chanted laughingly.

Ben huffed, pretending to be insulted. He crossed his arms, frowned, and slouched down in the throne. "Don't be ridiculous! I am an amazing king!" he informed them.

"Seems you have a mutiny on your hands, Benjamin." King Arthur laughed, walking into the room with Fidelis limping slowly beside him. "Only Fidelis seems to be your loyal subject. Maybe he thinks you're going to throw the scepter for him to fetch. I have to admit, however, that you look better with my crown and scepter than I do."

"Thanks, Your Majesty. At least Fido knows how to be a loyal subject. Unlike some people," Ben said, pointing the scepter toward Joseph and Sam.

"Hey, Your Majesty, that gives me an idea," Joseph said hopefully.

"Yes, Joseph?" King Arthur asked as Ben gave him back his crown and scepter and hopped off the throne.

"Could I borrow your crown and scepter until tomorrow? It'd be cool to dress up as

you for Halloween," Joseph said. "But only if you wouldn't mind."

"Wonderful idea," King Arthur replied. "The magic in these objects will help you to get home safely. The Black Knight's power is stronger on All Hallows' Eve, you know."

10

WEREWOLF PACK

Joseph, Sam, and Ben each hugged Fidelis good-bye.

"Right makes might, my young knights! Right makes might!" King Arthur called after them.

They followed True Heart through the woods as quickly as they could. King Arthur's scepter glowed to light the path in front of them. The woods were silent and creepy, but there was no sign of the werewolves, except tracks in the mud.

"Let's hope they went deeper into the

woods to hunt," Joseph gulped, holding the scepter tight and pushing the crown up, out of his eyes. It was a little big for him.

When they reached home, Sam helped Joseph over the fence, and then she and Ben climbed over.

"Oh, kids! I was so worried about you!" Mom ran to them from the house and flung her arms around them. "Is Fidelis doing okay?"

"He's doing great," Joseph answered.

Just then a hairy man jumped out from behind a tree.

"Werewolf!" Ben hollered.

Joseph dropped the scepter, and his borrowed crown fell off. Sam held up her shield.

"Wow, I must really have a great costume," Dad grinned, pulling off his shaggy

hood and spitting out his huge fake teeth. "I decided I'd be a werewolf with you, Ben. If Joseph dressed up, too, we could be a pack of werewolves. Your mom got this fake fur to glue to our faces and some goopy fake blood to put around our mouths. Cool, huh?"

"Now we know where you get that jumping-out-at-people thing." Joseph glared at Ben.

"Heh, heh," Ben laughed nervously. "Nice costume, Dad. You really had us fooled. But I was thinking I'd dress up as a zombie football player, like last year."

"What, no werewolf?" Dad asked, sharing a glance with Mom.

A wolf howled in the distance. All three kids jumped again.

"No, I don't want to be a werewolf anymore." Ben shook his head quickly. "Not after I almost became a real one," he added under his breath.

Joseph and Sam laughed as they followed him into the house.

Okay, Knights of Right, let's see if you've earned your armor. King Arthur has a few questions for you . . .

1. Why is it important to stand up to negative peer pressure? Have you ever stood up against peer pressure?
2. What is the best response if a friend tries to get you to drink or do something else dangerous?
3. How can you be a good friend and help others make good choices?
4. Why is it important to tell a parent, teacher, or principal if someone is doing something illegal or dangerous?
5. Why does King Arthur tell Joseph and Ben that knights need good friends?
6. What would you do if someone dared you to do something dangerous or illegal?
7. What would you do if friends started to destroy someone else's property?
8. What would you do if you saw some friends drinking? Why is teenage drinking wrong?

King Arthur asks—Did you know?

1. Long-term risks of drinking include liver damage, pancreatitis, certain cancers, and literal shrinkage of the brain (see www.teendrugabuse.us/teensandalcohol.html).
2. Young people can die from drinking alcohol. Every year in the United States some 5,000 young people under the age of twenty-one die of alcohol-related causes (see www.niaaa.nih.gov/AboutNIAAA/NIAAASponsoredPrograms/underage.htm#statistics).
3. The average age when youth first try alcohol is eleven for boys and thirteen for girls (see www.focusas.com/Alcohol.html).
4. Peer pressure is pressure from others to do something you don't want to do. This pressure can include put-downs, rejections, and false reasoning, as well as unspoken pressure. Being aware of the pressure is the first step to resisting it.
5. Almost everyone faces peer pressure once in a while. Friends have a big influence on our lives, but sometimes they push us to do things that we don't want to do. Here are some suggestions for dealing with negative peer pressure (see www.thecoolspot.gov/right2.asp):
   - Say no assertively.
   - Stay alcohol free.
   - Suggest something else to do.
   - Stand up for others.
   - Walk away from the situation.
   - Find something else to do with other friends.

Remember, Knights, right makes might. Keep making good choices and earning your armor!

King Arthur

ABOUT THE AUTHOR

M'Lin Rowley is seventeen years old and attends American Fork High School in Utah, where her mascot is a caveman rather than a knight. She loves snow skiing, rock climbing, going to movies with her friends, and writing stories. M'Lin hopes that people will enjoy her books and learn something from them.